Monica is a mother of two, grandmother of five and teacher of hundreds.

She still volunteers in schools and daycare centres, bringing the sound of music to the classroom – playing her guitar and singing with the children.

To Emma
Hugs
Moggie

SO HOW COME YOU HAVE TWO MOTHERS?

MONICA REILLY

AUSTIN MACAULEY PUBLISHERS™
LONDON • CAMBRIDGE • NEW YORK • SHARJAH

ISBN 9781398457430 (Paperback)
ISBN 9781398457447 (ePub-e-book)

www.austinmacauley.com

First Published 2022
Austin Macauley Publishers Ltd®
1 Canada Square
Canary Wharf
London
E14 5AA

I dedicate this book to my granddaughter
Jocelyn (Jossy)

I would like to thank Jackie Ressa for her artwork
and support.

"I dunno, I just do.
I guess I'm just lucky."

7

"What do you call your mums?"

"The shorter one is Mummy and the taller one is Mum."

"So who drives you to school? Who drives you to gymnastics?"

"Well...usually Mummy does 'cos my mum goes to work at the hospital early every morning."

"What's it like having two mums?"

"Well, we all love each other,
That's for sure."

"I don't know what is it like having a mum and a dad.
You have a mum and dad...right?"

13

"Yup! So how is your life different?"

"It isn't. We both have a family..."

"It's probably the same as us.
But we have a dog…"

"And we have a cat!"

"So I guess, we're pretty much the same!"

THE END